Express Yourself

From Here To There

Written by Ben Keckler

Illustrated by Dick Davis

Creative Development by Diana Barnard

Eagle Creek Publications
PO Box 781166
Indianapolis, Indiana 46278

This book is for the sojourners who teach us about the transitions **From Here To There**.
Special thanks to Al, Frank and Mom.
–B.K.

From Here To There
Text copyright © 2005 by Benjamin F. Keckler, III
Illustrations copyright © by Benjamin F. Keckler, III
Printed in the USA
Eagle Creek Publications, PO Box 781166, Indianapolis, Indiana 46278
www.eaglecreekpubs.com

Library of Congress Cataloguing-In-Publication Data
Keckler III, Benjamin F.
From Here To There/by Ben Keckler; illustrated by Dick Davis; artistic consultant Diana Barnard; 1st ed.
p.   cm.
Summary: A young man learns about life transitions, even dying,
by probing for answers he discovers are within himself.
ISBN 0-9769093-0-8
[1.Stories in rhyme 2. Self-help-Transition, Grief 3.Religion-Spirituality]

This book is dedicated to Christopher Morrison

This book is created especially for you by a whole team of people who want you to be the best you can be. Ben, Cheryl, Diana, Dick, Mike, Lori, Logan and Sean have come together to share Chris' journey From Here To There.

We're thinking of you!

This book belongs to

_____

Place your picture here

Tell me, tell me if you dare,
'Bout the journey from here to there.

The answers are within – just listen,
Soon you'll find your soul will glisten.

So, let's look inside your soul,
And explore your feelings, that's the goal.

When you name them, claim them, you will find,
The Holy One is faithful, loving and very kind.

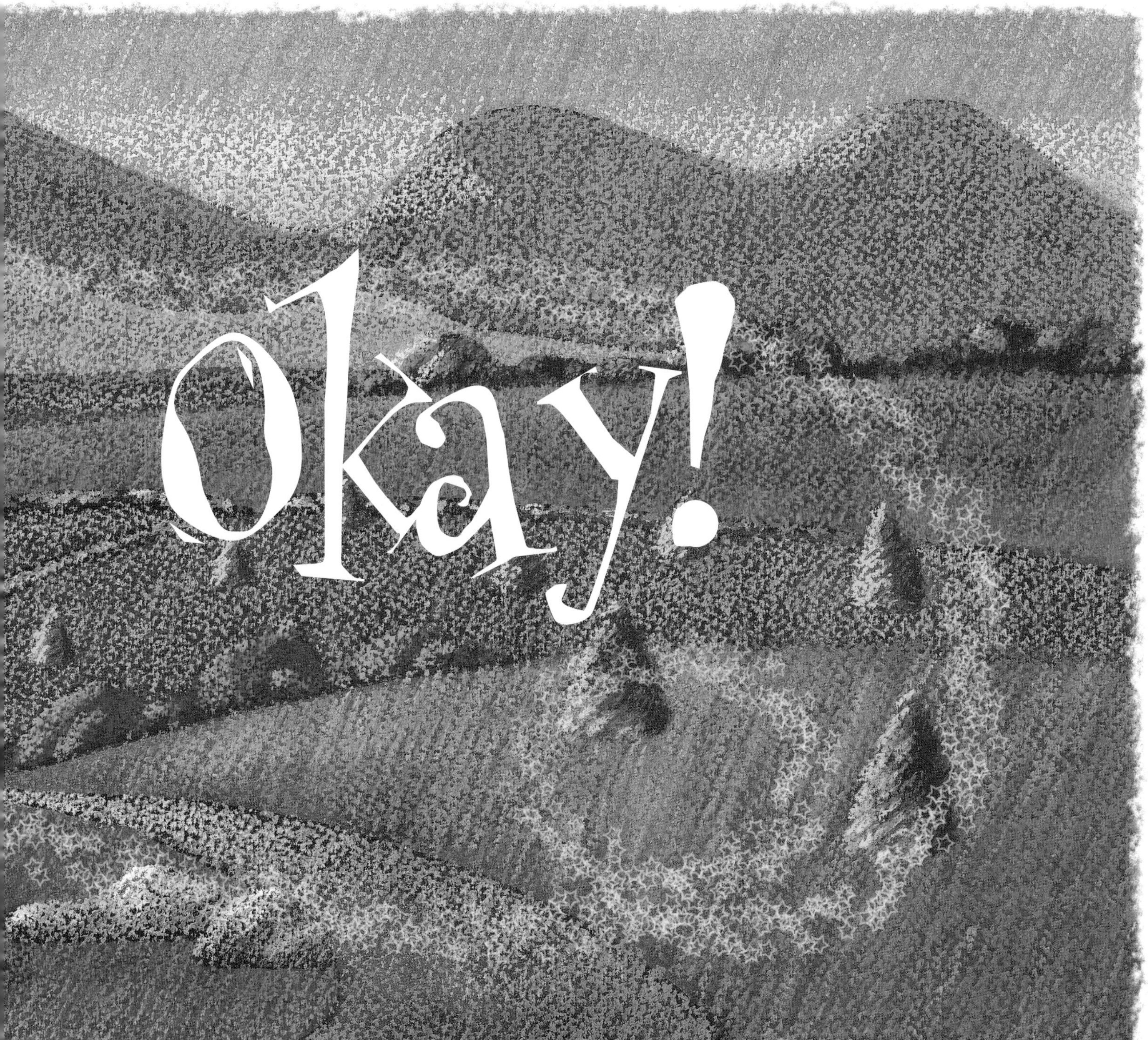
Okay!

Scared is one I feel today –
That's a good one I must say.

Mad is another feeling I know –
Then let it out or your top you'll blow.

Can you tell me about sad?

Yes I can – it isn't bad!

Wait! Glad and happy, they're in here too!
Opening to my feelings is so fresh and new!

What is this roller coaster – a nightmare?

Or is it part of my journey from here to there?

Wow! As I speak these things I feel,
I'm starting to sense God is real.

And something is on the increase –
Gosh! It's a feeling I call peace!

As I name the things inside,
There's no reason to run or hide.

What I'm learning about the eternal,
Comes when I get hold of things internal.

Yes! I'm finding there is nothing to fear.
God is much nearer than it might appear!

So if your heart is about to bust,

Remember the journey is all about trust!

Look deep down inside your soul,

There doesn't have to be a big black hole.

When you start your feelings to share,

You'll discover God's healing while you're unaware.

Soon you too will see there never was an end in sight,
Only to God's realm have I taken my flight.

Tell me, tell me if you dare,

`Bout the journey from here to there.

Express yourself !

It's your turn to express your feelings.

The child within each of us, regardless of age

There is a child within each of us longing to express our feelings.

The journey **From Here To There** is about every transition we encounter in life.

Transitions force us to examine our spiritual journey, and this is most evident in experiences

surrounding death and dying. Now is an excellent time to enjoy the feeling Chris expressed

the day he discovered, "Opening to my feelings is so fresh and new."

Draw a picture

Take some time to create a picture of your loved one *or*
create a picture of a special place where you want to encounter your loved one.

Symbols, Meaningful and Fun

A symbol is a visible expression of our feelings, our hopes and our dreams.

On the following pages you can create some special symbols that will help you embrace

your memories, recall stories and connect with your emotions. Creating

symbolic connections might enable you to discover, like Chris did, "For what I'm learning

about the eternal, comes when I get hold of things internal."

Here's a familiar symbol:

XOXOXO

Do you recognize it? If not, we bet someone you know will tell you!

We chose a star and a spiral as special symbols for this book.

You choose whatever symbols you feel! Remember the key is "Express Yourself!"

Create your story about your loved one

Try creating a story or a "name poem" about your loved one

using the letters of their name to begin each line. Or listen to

your heart about other creative ways to tell the story you feel.

Create a dream catcher

What is a dream catcher? Native Americans created dream catchers to help them with their dreams, believing that their good dreams would pass through the center and reach them and that their bad dreams would get caught in the webbing of the dream catcher.

They kept them close to where they slept.

Let's try making a dream catcher. If you want to visit our website (www.eaglecreekpubs) and order our **From Here To There** art kit, it contains everything you'll need, except the scissors.

If you want to pick up your own materials, here is what you'll need:

1. Any size or type of wooden or plastic ring or even an embroidery hoop

2. About 2 yards of string, ribbon or yarn

3. Any kind of beads and feathers

4. A pencil

1. Make eight marks (about the same distance apart) around the ring.

3. Continue to knot the string at the other seven marks, so that the string is loose between the loops.

2. Tie a knot at one mark and leave about 3 inches of string to use in step 5.

4. Continue to loop the string so that it looks like a web, maybe adding a bead or beads as you make your web. When you have a small hole left in the center, make a knot so your web doesn't unravel.

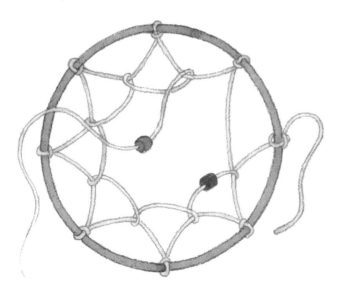

5. Take the extra string from step 2 and tie it in a knot to your web. Now your web is secure on each end. Make a loop and attach it for hanging. Add feathers and beads as you like.

Create a treasure box

These are pictures of some treasure boxes we've created at ECP. You may want to create your own. It can be simple or fancy. It can be created in a shoe box or a special box from a craft shop. Just find small objects that remind you of your loved one and place them in the box using *your* creative genius.

Below are some questions that may help you get started. We realize they may take you to some difficult places in your grief journey; our prayer is for you to do this activity trusting that healing will continue to come to you and those you love.

1. The name of your loved one. Any nicknames?
2. Birthdate and age of loved one at their death. Other significant dates?
3. Relationship to your loved one.
4. Think of what would best characterize your loved one, or something the recipient, if someone other than yourself, would use to characterize your loved one.
5. One item, theme, "representation of," or common interest that may be only understood between the receiver of the treasure box and your loved one.
6. Your loved one's likes, dislikes, and favorites. Possibilities might include (but not limited to) places, activities, sports, phrases, foods, art, colors, hobbies, symbols, dreams, life goals, styles of music, clothing, décor.
7. You might want to write something on the bottom of the box. Possibilities might include a quote, date, brief message, to/from.

What is normal?

Sometimes grief, loss and transition cause us to ask, "What is normal?"
Here are some things you might experience on your journey **From Here To There**.

FEELINGS
- Sadness
- Shock
- Anger
- Guilt and self-reproach
- Denial
- Anxiety and fear
- Loneliness and desolation
- Helplessness
- Yearning
- Relief
- Release
- Numbness
- Disorientation

PHYSICAL SENSATIONS
- Emptiness in the chest or stomach
- Tightness in the throat or chest
- Breathlessness
- Weakness in the muscles
- Lack of energy
- Headaches and backaches
- Stomach problems
- Dry mouth
- Skin problems
- Insomnia
- Minor weight loss
- A sense of depersonalization: "I walk down the street and nothing seems real, including myself."

COGNITION/THOUGHTS
- Disbelief
- Confusion
- Preoccupation with thoughts about the deceased
- Sense of presence of the dead
- Hallucination—both the visual and the auditory types

BEHAVIORS
- Sleep disturbances
- Appetite disturbances
- Absent-minded behavior
- Social withdrawal/Dreams of the deceased
- Avoiding reminders of the deceased
- Searching and calling out
- Sighing
- Overactivity
- Crying
- Visiting places or carrying objects that remind one of the deceased

Reaction page

We wouldn't be surprised if you've got some creative juices flowing inside of you as you
journey **From Here To There**. We are leaving this page especially for you.
Use it in your special way to express yourself. We hope you'll feel surrounded with
everything you need for your journey and, if you want to tell us about what you've created,
drop us a note at Eagle Creek Publications, PO Box 781166, Indianapolis, IN 46278
or visit us on the web at www.eaglecreekpubs.com

Remember...

"Express Yourself on your journey
From Here To There!"